caillou®

watches Rosie

Adaptation from the animated series: Marion Johnson
Illustrations: CINAR Animation and adapted by Éric Sévigny

chouette **CINAR®**

Caillou and Rosie are playing with Rosie's new toy.

They are having lots of fun—lots of noisy fun!

Every time Rosie pushes a key, the toy makes an animal sound.

MOO! QUACK! ARF!

MEOW!

Mommy calls to them, "Children, you're making too much noise."

Caillou and Rosie stop what they are doing.

"Caillou, I need to lie down," says Mommy. "Can you be a good big brother and watch Rosie so she doesn't get into mischief?"

"Yes, Mommy," Caillou replies.

Mommy brings a couple of markers and two big pieces of paper.

"You and Rosie can draw pictures of the animals instead of listening to the sounds they make," she tells Caillou.

"I need you to play quietly so I can rest."

"Okay," says Caillou.

Caillou wants to help Mommy. He wants to be a good big brother.

Caillou hands Rosie a marker and says, "We're going to draw now."

Caillou starts drawing a giraffe. He works so hard on his picture, he doesn't notice that Rosie is not drawing beside him.

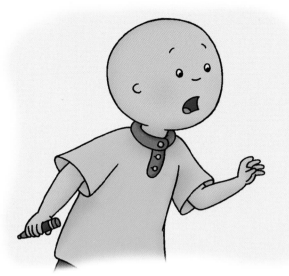

Caillou looks around to see where Rosie went.

Oh, no! Rosie is drawing on the wall!

"Rosie! No!" shouts Caillou.

Caillou grabs the marker away from Rosie.

"No! No! Mine!" cries Rosie, and tries to get it back.

Caillou holds on to the marker. Rosie starts to cry.

"Be quiet!" Caillou tells her. "Do you want Mommy to get mad?"

Mommy hears all the noise.

"Caillou," Mommy says, picking up Rosie, "I asked you to be a good big brother and watch Rosie, not fight with her. Rosie needs her nap. I'll be right back."

Caillou is suprised. Why is Mommy angry with him?

He did his best to be quiet and to keep Rosie from doing anything wrong.

He doesn't want to be Rosie's big brother any more!

When Mommy comes back, Caillou is crying.

Caillou and Mommy go to the kitchen and fill a pail with soap and water.

Mommy says, "It isn't easy being a big brother, is it?"

Caillou shakes his head. "Can I help?" he asks.

Mommy nods. "That would be great, Caillou."

Caillou cleans the wall with a wet cloth.

He rubs hard until all the marks are gone.

"Good work, Caillou! Thank you," says Mommy.

Rosie is finished her nap, and she wants Caillou to play with her.
Caillou smiles and says, "Okay, Rosie!"
Mommy gives Caillou a hug.
"Caillou, you are becoming such a big boy," she says. "And you
are such a good big brother to Rosie!"

Text adapted by Marion Johnson from the scenario of the CAILLOU animated film series
produced by CINAR Corporation (© 1997 Caillou Productions Inc., a subsidiary of
CINAR Corporation). All rights reserved.
Original story written by Christel Kleitch.
Illustrations taken from the television series CAILLOU and adapted by Éric Sévigny.
Art Direction: Monique Dupras

Canadian Cataloguing in Publication Data

Johnson, Marion, 1949-
Caillou watches Rosie
(Playtime)
For children aged 3 and up.
Co-published by: CINAR Corporation.

ISBN 2-89450-326-1

1. Brothers and sisters – Juvenile literature.   2. Babysitting – Juvenile
literature.   I. CINAR Corporation.   II. Title.   III. Series: Playtime
(Montreal, Quebec).

BF723.S43J63 2002   j306.875   C2002-940368-5

Legal deposit: 2002

We gratefully acknowledge the financial support of
BPIDP and SODEC for our publishing activities.

Printed in Canada
10 9 8 7 6 5 4 3 2 1